my itty-bitty bio

Lady Bird Johnson

Published in the United States of America by Cherry Lake Publishing Group
Ann Arbor, Michigan
www.cherrylakepublishing.com

Reading Adviser: Marla Conn, MS Ed., Literacy specialist, Read-Ability, Inc.
Book Designer: Jennifer Wahi
Illustrator: Jeff Bane

Photo Credits: ©LBJ Library photo by Unknown/Serial No. B9742, 5; ©LBJ Library photo by Unknown/Serial No. B2686, 7; ©LBJ Library photo by Unknown/Serial No. B7029-3, 9; ©LBJ Library photo by Yoichi Okamoto/Serial No. A6608-30a, 11, 22; ©LBJ Library photo by Yoichi Okamoto/Serial No. W13-2, 13; ©LBJ Library photo by Robert Knudsen/Serial No. D782-9A, 15; ©LBJ Library photo by Robert Knudsen/Serial No. C9080-17A, 17; ©LBJ Library photo by Frank Wolfe/Serial No. D7682-28A, 19, 23; ©LBJ Library photo by Frank Muto/Serial No. 58-8-18, 21; Jeff Bane, Cover, 1, 8, 10, 12

Cherry Lake Press is an imprint of Cherry Lake Publishing Group.

Library of Congress Cataloging-in-Publication Data

Names: Pincus, Meeg, author. | Bane, Jeff, 1957- illustrator.
Title: Lady Bird Johnson / Meeg Pincus ; illustrated by Jeff Bane.
Description: Ann Arbor, Michigan : Cherry Lake Publishing, 2021. | Series: My itty-bitty bio | Includes index. | Audience: Grades K-1 | Summary: “The My Itty-Bitty Bio series are biographies for the earliest readers. This book examines the life former First Lady Claudia Alta “Lady Bird” Alta Johnson in a simple, age-appropriate way that will help young readers develop word recognition and reading skills. Includes a table of contents, author biography, timeline, glossary, index, and other informative backmatter”-- Provided by publisher.
Identifiers: LCCN 2020035901 (print) | LCCN 2020035902 (ebook) | ISBN 9781534179950 (hardcover) | ISBN 9781534181663 (paperback) | ISBN 9781534180963 (pdf) | ISBN 9781534182677 (ebook)
Subjects: LCSH: Johnson, Lady Bird, 1912-2007--Juvenile literature. | Presidents’ spouses--United States--Biography--Juvenile literature.
Classification: LCC E848.J64 P56 2021 (print) | LCC E848.J64 (ebook) | DDC 973.923092 [B]--dc23
LC record available at https://lccn.loc.gov/2020035901
LC ebook record available at https://lccn.loc.gov/2020035902

Printed in the United States of America
Corporate Graphics

table of contents

About the author: Meeg Pincus has been a writer, editor, and educator for 25 years. She loves to write inspiring stories for kids about people, animals, and our planet. She lives near San Diego, California, where she enjoys the beach, reading, singing, and her family.

About the illustrator: Jeff Bane and his two business partners own a studio along the American River in Folsom, California, home of the 1849 Gold Rush. When Jeff's not sketching or illustrating for clients, he's either swimming or kayaking in the river to relax.

I was born in Texas. It was 1912.
I had two older brothers.

My mother died when I was 5.

Playing in the woods made me happy.

What makes you happy
when you're sad?

I went to college. I studied history. Then, I met Lyndon B. Johnson. We got married. I worked in **politics** with him.

My husband became president of the United States. This meant I became the **First Lady**. I was 51. President Kennedy had died. I helped comfort the country.

I helped protect **nature**.
I helped clean up cities.
I added wildflowers along
America's roads.

What do you like about nature?

I traveled to America's **national parks**. I helped pass over 200 **conservation** laws.

I also helped children living in **poverty**. I supported a preschool program called Head Start.

NO
PARKING

I opened the Wildflower Center in Texas. It has gardens to visit and **programs** for kids.

I died at age 94. I accomplished many things. My Wildflower Center lives on. So does the work I did for nature and children.

What would you like to ask me?

1963

1910

Born
1912

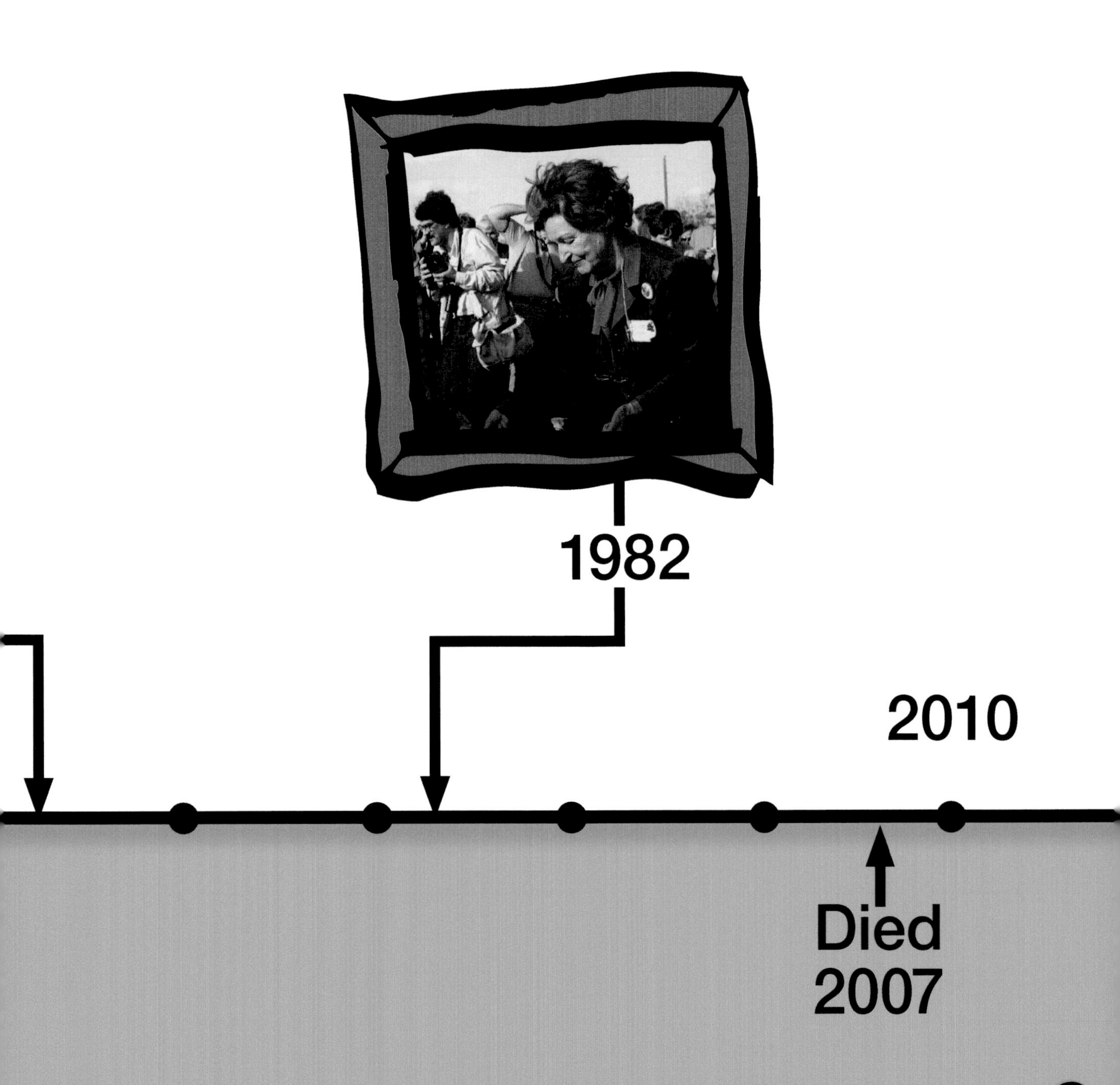
1982
2010
Died
2007

glossary & index

glossary

conservation (kahn-sur-VAY-shuhn) the protection of things in nature like wildlife and forests

first lady (FURST LAY-dee) the wife of the president of the United States

national parks (NASH-uh-nuhl PAHRKS) large areas of natural land protected by the government for people to visit

nature (NAY-chur) things in the world not made by people, like animals, plants, and the weather

politics (PAH-lih-tiks) the activities done to govern a countr

poverty (PAH-vur-tee) the state of being poor or not having enough to live on

programs (PROH-gramz) lessons or events

index